To my sons, Sam and Ford —A.R.

For Mom —K.K.

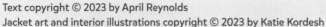

Text copyright © 2023 by April Reynolds
Jacket art and interior illustrations copyright © 2023 by Katie Kordesh

All rights reserved. Published in the United States by Anne Schwartz Books, an imprint of Random House Children's Books, a division of Penguin Random House LLC, New York.

Anne Schwartz Books and the colophon are trademarks of Penguin Random House LLC.

Visit us on the Web! rhcbooks.com

Educators and librarians, for a variety of teaching tools, visit us at RHTeachersLibrarians.com

Library of Congress Cataloging-in-Publication Data is available upon request.
ISBN 978-0-593-56460-8 (trade) — ISBN 978-0-593-56461-5 (lib. bdg.) —
ISBN 978-0-593-56462-2 (ebook)

The text of this book is set in 15.5-point Mikado.
The illustrations were rendered in ink and watercolor.
Book design by Taline Boghosian

MANUFACTURED IN CHINA   10 9 8 7 6 5 4 3 2 1   First Edition

SAM WITH ANTS IN HIS PANTS

written by
April Reynolds

illustrated by
Katie Kordesh

a·s·b

anne schwartz books

One afternoon, right before nap time,
Sam's mother told him he had ants in his pants
and, really, he must settle down.

Which is just when he ran down the hall, shouting, "Yeeeee!"

"Bedtime for a short time!
And that means now," Momma said.

"Noooo!"

Sam cried, flew to his room . . .

. . . and slammed the door shut tight.

He threw open his favorite book, *African Wildlife*.
And when he opened this most magical book . . .

. . . it came alive and a herd of gazelles jumped right off the pages.

Woop, Woop, Woop!

"Shh," Sam said.
"Momma says it's nap time."

But Sam couldn't stop the pride of lions from stalking off page eleven and hiding under his bed.

ROAR!

A zeal of zebras, a little less noisy,
was right behind.

A troop of baboons bounded off page twenty-two.

Hoo! Hoo!

They smacked their lips and narrowed their eyes and kept their ears back. Sam knew, from listening to Momma read page twenty-three, that this meant they wanted to be friends.

"Hello," Sam said.

A tower of giraffes strode from his favorite
(shh, that's a secret) page and began to

snore and snort,
hiss and whistle.

Yes, giraffes *are* rather talkative.

A bloat of hippos took a swipe at his toy spaceship.

A parade of elephants, who sadly can't run,
walked very quickly past Snuggle Rabbit.

And one single cheetah prowled over to Sam's backpack, for as he knew, cheetahs travel alone.

How could Sam *ever* be expected to take a nap?

Especially with a charm of hummingbirds
hovering around his night-light . . .

A leap of leopards
dancing on the rug . . .

A crash of rhinoceroses
enjoying the soles of his shoes.

Finally, amid all the jumping and stalking and bounding and striding and swiping and walking very quickly and prowling and hovering and dancing and enjoying came a sound louder than any other.

GRROOWWL

it went.

It was the sound of Sam's tummy.
And it scared those ants right out of his pants.

Then Sam yawned and went to look for Momma.

There she was,
at the kitchen table,
along with his dinner.

And like the best little boys,
even the ones with ants in their pants . . .

. . . Sam decided to share.

And there was plenty to go around.